CELEBRATING
AMERICA

CELEBRATING AMERICA

A Collection of Poems and Images of the American Spirit

Poetry compiled by Laura Whipple

Art provided by The Art Institute of Chicago

PHILOMEL BOOKS   NEW YORK

In Association With

THE ART INSTITUTE OF CHICAGO

Jacket art:

Winslow Homer (American, 1836–1910)
''For to Be a Farmer's Boy'', 1887
Watercolor over pencil on paper, 14 × 20 in.
Anonymous gift in memory of Edward Carson Waller, 1963.760

Philomel Books, a division of The Putnam & Grosset Group,
200 Madison Avenue, New York, NY 10016.
Philomel Books, Reg. U.S. Pat. & Tm. Off.
Published simultaneously in Canada.
Printed in Hong Kong by South China Printing Co. (1988) Ltd.
Book design by Jackie Schuman.
The text is set in Meridien.

Library of Congress Cataloging-in-Publication Data

Celebrating America : a collection of poems and images of the American
    spirit / poetry compiled by Laura Whipple ; art provided by the Art
    Institute of Chicago.
        p.   cm.
    Includes bibliographical references and indexes.
    Summary: Expressions of American life by Whitman, Riley, Field,
Longfellow, Dunbar, folk sources, Indian tribes and a host of
others.
        1. America—Juvenile poetry.   2. Children's poetry, American.
3. United States—Juvenile poetry.   4. America in art—Juvenile
literature.   5. United States in art—Juvenile literature.
[1. United States—Poetry.   2. American poetry—Collections.]
I. Whipple, Laura.   II. Art Institute of Chicago.
PS595.A43C44   1994
811.008′03273—dc20   92-26197   CIP   AC r93
ISBN 0-399-22036-4

10 9 8 7 6 5 4 3 2 1
First Impression

Contents

Introduction, Laura Whipple 7

LAND

That Mountain Far Away / *Tewa* 11
Volcano / *Ivan Van Sertima* 12
A Spell of Weather / *Eve Merriam* 13
Song for Smooth Waters / *Haida* 14
Last summer . . . / *Eleanor Schick* 15
Zimmer in Fall / *Paul Zimmer* 16
Snow-Flakes / *Henry Wadsworth Longfellow* 17
There was a mountain, over its black roots [the deer] . . . / *Papago* 17
A Country Pathway / *James Whitcomb Riley* 18

STORIES

Inscription on the Liberty Bell / *Book of Leviticus* 21
The Statue of Old Andrew Jackson / *Vachel Lindsay* 22
Abraham Lincoln / *Mildred Meigs* 23
Paul Revere's Ride / *Henry Wadsworth Longfellow* 24
The Flower-Fed Buffalos / *Vachel Lindsay* 25
Magic Formula / *Iroquois* 26
Cowboy Sayings 27
Texas Cowboy Song 27
The New Colossus / *Emma Lazarus* 28
Both My Grandmothers / *Edward Field* 29
Pioneers / *Aileen Fisher and Olive Rabe* 30

HEART

Thanksgiving Dinner / *Aileen Fisher* 33
Train Is A-comin' / *American Folksong* 34
Four of July / *Robert Newton Peck* 35
A Boy's Summer / *Paul Laurence Dunbar* 36
A Railroad Man for Me / *American Folksong* 37
I had a little mule and his name was Jack . . . / *American Nursery Rhyme* 37
My Dad / *Laura Whipple* 38
City Baseball / *Liz Rosenberg* 39
Brooklyn Bridge / *William Jay Smith* 40
The Foundations of American Industry / *Donald Hall* 41
The Bridge / *Charlotte Zolotow* 41
Smoke Animals / *Rowena Bastin Bennett* 42
People Who Must / *Carl Sandburg* 43
door / *Valerie Worth* 44
Midwest Town / *Ruth Delong Peterson* 45
Hang Out the Flag / *James S. Tippett* 46
Our Flag 47
Map of My Country / *John Holmes* 48

PEOPLE

trips / *Nikki Giovanni 51*
To P.J. (2 yrs old who sed write a poem for me in Portland, Oregon) / *Sonia Sanchez 52*
Narcissa / *Gwendolyn Brooks 53*
Four on a Sidewalk / *American Counting Rhyme 53*
The Weary Blues / *Langston Hughes 54*
Motto / *Langston Hughes 55*
The true storyteller is a . . . / *Toltec 56*
The Toltecs were wise . . . / *Toltec 57*
A voice . . . / *Teton Sioux 57*
Song of the Broad-Axe, 3 / *Walt Whitman 58*
Dream Song / *Chippewa 59*
The Ploughman / *Oliver Wendell Holmes 60*
Sailor Boy's Song / *American Sailing Song 61*
It takes a mighty fire . . . / *H. D. Carberry 62*

SPIRIT

And Yet the Earth Remains Unchanged / *Aztec 65*
Shirt / *Carl Sandburg 66*
Help! / *X. J. Kennedy 67*
In the Evening / *Siv Cedering 68*
At Dawn / *Michael Patrick Hearn 69*
Three/Quarters Time / *Nikki Giovanni 70*
Circles / *Harry Behn 71*
Red / *Eugene Field 71*
Why? / *Myra Cohn Livingston 72*
Hurt / *Marcie Hans 73*
Keep a Hand on Your Dream / *X. J. Kennedy 74*

Index of First Lines 75
Index of Poets and Artists 76
Notes on the Artwork 77
Acknowledgments 79

Introduction

There is much in America to celebrate: a glittering bridge, a volcano, a three-quarter-time dance, a small town, the Fourth of July, an immigrant grandmother, a beautiful little brother or sister, factories, farms, skyscrapers, prairies, cowboys, and Abraham Lincoln—all threads in the fabric of the American spirit. American art and poetry can speak eloquently about what America is, creating specific images that allow the American spirit to be seen and heard and experienced. *Celebrating America* is a weaving of these images for children.

Just as the material of a small American town is woven of varied voices with individual histories, we need to honor the varied voices that have created America. It is not the scope of this collection to be inclusive of each historical era, each variety of people, each phenomenon of nature that has shaped America. *Celebrating America* is a sampler, a little this, a little that, a pastiche of art and poetry that represents the uniqueness of the American spirit.

How can we describe the spirit of America? An adult may see in this joining of American art and poetry a web of intertwining questions. (A metaphor for America?) What power does the land have over what America has been and is becoming? How do stories of the past suggest turmoil and loss, and yet renewal? Why does the substance of individual lives speak to the heart of all? Can the people in their increasing diversity be, in one voice, the truest story-tellers of America? Why do disparate strands of joy and sorrow, humor and hurt, confidence and uncertainty, stoic acceptance and the tenacious pursuit of a dream combine to spin a fabric uniquely American?

These abstractions circle round and are largely inaccessible to children. Young children are visual, not intellectual. They first react to what they see. What will the child see in the art? What part of the image will pull the child in? Children's life experiences are intense, indelible. They have no training in the visual arts, no art history courses to explain and amplify. They have to be able to relate some element in the art to their own experiences; to put themselves in the picture and try it on. The same is true of the poetry. Children relate eagerly to ideas and the intriguing or beautiful use of language in poetry, to specific images, to feelings those images evoke. A child is not too young to experience small epiphanies. *Celebrating America* is an illumination of art with words and an illustrating of the words with art for the child, who will move from one to the other, and come to an understanding beyond the words or images alone.

This visual and verbal patchwork evocative of America is rich with shifting varieties of style. This is as it should be. From the flowing language of

Longfellow to the pithy humor of X. J. Kennedy, from the classical landscapes of George Inness to the vibrant abstractions of Jackson Pollock, it seems apparent that complementary opposites, like diversity and universality, inter-woven with hope, are the major threads in the tapestry called the American spirit. As H. D. Carberry says in "It takes a mighty fire . . ."

> The mould is not yet made, perhaps,
> that can unite and make the people one.
> But more important than the mould
> is the temper of the steel,
> the spirit of the people.

The American spirit is ever evolving. It will always be so.

Laura Whipple
October 1993

LAND

Niagara Falls, 1830
Thomas Cole

THAT MOUNTAIN FAR AWAY

My home over there, my home over there,
My home over there, now I remember it!
And when I see that mountain far away,
Why, then I weep. Alas! What can I do? . . .
My home over there, now I remember it.

Tewa

Cotopaxi, 1857
Frederic Edwin Church

VOLCANO

When I speak, now,
there are no urgent rumblings in my voice;
no scarlet vapour issues from my lips;
I spit no lava;
But I am a volcano, . . .
When I speak, now,
no one can hear me;
the thunder lies too deep, too deep,
for violent cataclysm. . . .
Time heaps high snow on my passive body
and I stand muted, with my furnace caged,
too chilled for agitation.
But mark me, well,
for I am still a volcano; . . .

Ivan Van Sertima
1971

A SPELL OF WEATHER

Begone, calm.
Come, zephyr.
Blow, breeze.
All hail, hail, cloudburst, torrent.

Grow, wind, into gust, squall, williwaw;
Spout, tempest, typhoon, gale,
Roar, tornado;
Rip, hurricane, rage, tide!

Then, spent,
Subside;
Beached . . .

Skies clearing,
Cerulean,
Unrippled blue.

Eve Merriam
1964

Factory Butte, Utah, 1975
William Clift

SONG FOR SMOOTH WATERS

Ocean Spirit
Calm the waves for me
get close to me, my power
my heart is tired
make the sea like milk for me
YEHO
YEHOLO

Haida

The Coast of Labrador, 1866
William Bradford

A Holiday, 1915
Edward Potthast

Last summer
when we went
to the seashore
I saw the water
rounding its back
and shouting
at the beach
where the people
were resting
like statues
in the sand.

Eleanor Schick
1974

Yellow Hickory Leaves with Daisy, 1928
Georgia O'Keeffe

ZIMMER IN FALL

Birds and leaves disconnect in Fall
But I hang on. Not one flower
Has to open for my happiness.
I am content in this season
Of retreat, finished with growth,
With striving and sorting.
I do not want even one cell
To stir and split.
Let it all stand as it is.

Paul Zimmer
1976

SNOW-FLAKES

Out of the bosom of the air,
      Out of the cloud-folds of her garments shaken,
Over the woodland brown and bare,
      Silent, and soft, and slow
      Descends the snow.

Henry Wadsworth Longfellow
1893

Icebound, 1889/1900
John Henry Twachtman

Mount Equinox, Winter, 1921
Rockwell Kent

There was a mountain, over its black roots [the deer]
      jumped and in front of it danced, and behind a grey
      mountain it stood.

Papago

Our Old Mill, 1849
George Inness

A COUNTRY PATHWAY

I come upon it suddenly, alone—
    A little pathway winding in the
       weeds
That fringe the roadside; and with
      dreams my own,
    I wander as it leads.

Full wistfully along the slender way,
    Through summer tan of freckled
      shade and shine,
I take the path that leads me as it
      may—
    Its every choice is mine.

James Whitcomb Riley
late nineteenth century

STORIES

INSCRIPTION ON THE LIBERTY BELL

  . . . proclaim liberty throughout
all the land
unto all the inhabitants
thereof.

The Book of Leviticus 25:10.

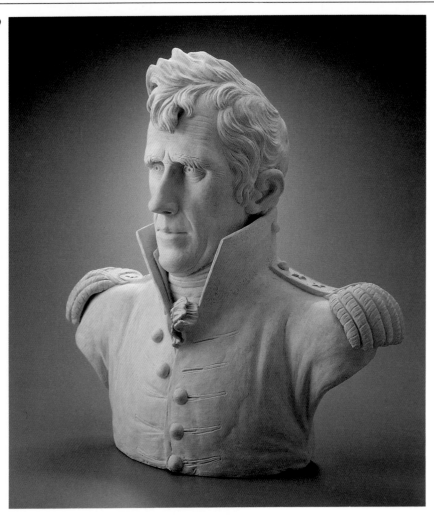

General Andrew Jackson, 1819
William Rush

THE STATUE OF OLD ANDREW JACKSON

Andrew Jackson was eight feet tall.
His arm was a hickory limb and a maul.
His sword was so long he dragged it on the ground.
Every friend was an equal. Every foe was a hound. . . .

He licked the British at Noo Orleans;
Beat them out of their elegant jeans.
He piled the cotton-bales twenty feet high,
And he snorted ''freedom'' and it flashed from his eye.

And the American Eagle swooped through the air,
And cheered when he heard the Jackson swear—
''By the Eternal, let them come.
Sound Yankee Doodle. Let the bullets hum.'' . . .

Vachel Lindsay
1920

ABRAHAM LINCOLN

Remember he was poor and country-bred;
His face was lined; he walked with awkward gait.
Smart people laughed at him sometimes and said,
''How can so very plain a man be great?''

Remember he was humble, used to toil.
Strong arms he had to build a shack, a fence,
Long legs to tramp the woods, to plow the soil,
A head chuck full of backwoods common sense. . . .

Remember that his eyes could light with fun;
That wisdom, courage, set his name apart;
But when the rest is duly said and done,
Remember that men loved him for his heart.

Mildred Meigs
1936

Lincoln, 1958
Robert Rauschenberg

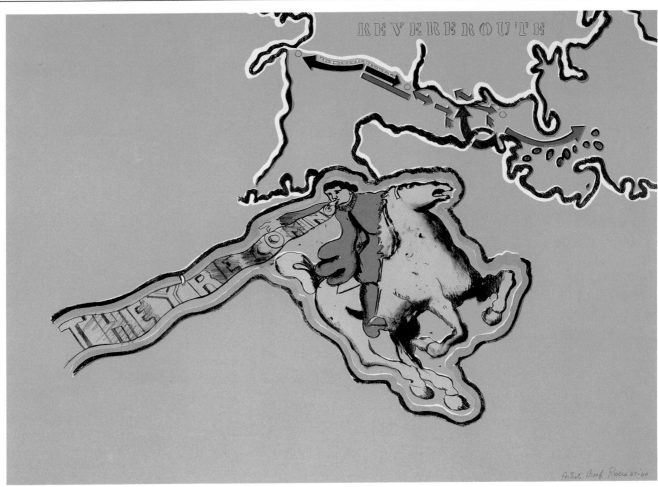

Once More Paul Revere, I, 1967–69
Larry Rivers

from: PAUL REVERE'S RIDE

So through the night rode Paul Revere;
And so through the night went his cry of alarm
To every Middlesex village and farm.

A cry of defiance and not of fear,
A voice in the darkness, a knock at the door,
And a word that shall echo forever more!

For, borne on the night-wind of the Past,
Through all our history, to the last,
In the hour of darkness and peril and need,

The people will waken and listen and hear
The hurrying hoof-beats of that steed,
And the midnight message of Paul Revere.

Henry Wadsworth Longfellow
1863

THE FLOWER-FED BUFFALOS

The flower-fed buffalos of the spring
In the days of long ago,
Ranged where the locomotives sing
And the prairie flowers lie low;
The tossing, blooming, perfumed grass
Is swept away by wheat,
Wheels and wheels and wheels spin by
In the spring that still is sweet.
But the flower-fed buffalos of the spring
Left us long ago.
They gore no more, they bellow no more,
They trundle around the hills no more;
With the Blackfeet lying low,
With the Pawnees lying low.

Vachel Lindsay
1926

Panel depicting Indians and Buffalo, mid-1850s
United States

Nothing But Cheerful Looks Followed the Bat, 1905
Frederic Remington

MAGIC FORMULA

You have no right to trouble me,
Depart, I am becoming stronger.
You are now departing from me,
You who would devour me;
I am becoming stronger, stronger.
Mighty medicine is now within me,
You cannot now subdue me—
I am becoming stronger,
I am stronger, stronger, stronger.

Iroquois

COWBOY SAYINGS

Most gunmen
wiggle their
trigger fingers
once too often.

By the rules of gunfighting,
the loser is wrong.

Bein' too positive in your opinions
kin get you invited to a dance in the street,
to the music of shots, nicely aimed.

The man who keeps a bridle on his temper
shoots the truest.

Savvy Sayin's
nineteenth century

O I'm a jolly old cowboy,
Just off the Texas Plains.
My trade is cinching saddles,
And pulling bridle reins.
It's I can throw a lasso
With the greatest ease,
And mount my bronco pony,
And ride him when I please!

Texas Cowboy Song
nineteenth century

Coming Through the Rye, modeled 1902, cast 1902–09
Frederic Remington

THE NEW COLOSSUS
(Inscription on the Statue of Liberty)

Not like the brazen giant of Greek fame,
 With conquering limbs astride from land to land;
 Here at our sea-washed, sunset gates shall stand
A mighty woman with a torch, whose flame
Is the imprisoned lightning, and her name
 Mother of Exiles. From her beacon-hand
 Glows world-wide welcome; . . .
I lift my lamp beside the golden door!

Emma Lazarus
1903

Statue of Liberty, date unknown
Margaret Bourke–White

Italian Family Seeking Lost Baggage, Ellis Island, 1905
Lewis Hine

BOTH MY GRANDMOTHERS

Both my grandmas came from far away
on the difficult journey alone with their children.
They had the courage to do that
but only enough strength
to get here, raise their kids, and die.
I myself have stood on the shore of the Caspian Sea
crying my eyes out
and knowing how far away far can be
and how far this America—strange and difficult even for me—
was from their homes,
from the life they yearned back to.
But they lived here uprooted the rest of their lives.

Edward Field
1977

Mount Washington, 1869
Winslow Homer

PIONEERS

Clothed in buckskin, clothed in homespun,
Clothed in strength and courage, too,
They pressed westward ever westward,
Where the land was wild and new.
Pioneers!

Wearing coonskin, wearing gingham,
Wearing patience mile on mile,
They crossed rivers, prairies, mountains,
Pressing westward all the while.
Pioneers!

Toting rifles, toting kettles,
Toting faith and hardihood,
They left comfort far behind them
For a future they thought good.
Pioneers!

They took little of the riches
That a wealthy man can boast,
But their courage, patience, vision,
Were the coins that matter most.
Pioneers!

Aileen Fisher and Olive Rabe
1956

HEART

Thanksgiving, 1935
Doris Lee

THANKSGIVING DINNER

With company coming,
there's always *before:*
shine up the silver,
sweep up the floor,
corn and red peppers
to hang by the door,
salad to garnish
and water to pour,
sample the dressing
and gravy once more . . .
Listen!
They're coming!
Oh, run to the door!

Aileen Fisher
1969

Train Station, 1936
Walter W. Ellison

TRAIN IS A-COMIN'

Train is a-comin', oh yes,
Train is a-comin', oh yes,
Train is a-comin', oh yes,
Train is a-comin', oh yes,
Train is a-comin', oh yes!

Better get your ticket, oh yes,
Better get your ticket, oh yes,
Better get your ticket, oh yes,
Better get your ticket, oh yes,
Better get your ticket, oh yes!

Stopping at the station, oh yes,
Stopping at the station, oh yes,
Stopping at the station, oh yes,
Stopping at the station, oh yes,
Stopping at the station, oh yes!

American Folksong
nineteenth century

Fourth of July Picnic at Weymouth Landing, c. 1853
Susan Merritt

FOUR OF JULY

We hitched up the mare and we buckled her down,
Piled in the buggy and headed for town.
We got to a spot that was covered with shade.
Somebody shouted, ''Here comes the parade!''

Potato sack races and kites on the fly,
A pie-eating contest with blueberry pie.
Baskets of picnics laid out in the park,
Awaiting the fireworks when it got dark.

Skyrockets wounding the heaven we saw,
Gasping the wonder and bursting with awe,
Standing stock still in the crowd and its stare
As white Roman candles would sparkle the air.

That beautiful day was so wonderful big,
That I slept the way home in the back of the rig,
And dreamed of Old Glory against a blue sky.
God surely hallowed the Four of July.

Robert Newton Peck
1975

A BOY'S SUMMER

With a line and hook
By a babbling brook,
The fisherman's sport we ply;
And list the song
of the feathered throng
That flits in the branches nigh.
At last we strip
For a quiet dip;
Ah, that is the best of joy.
For this I say
On a summer's day,
What's so fine as being a boy?
Ha, Ha!

Paul Laurence Dunbar
late nineteenth century

Wheatfield, 1940
Torvald Arnt Hoyer

Rug depicting Steam Engine, 19th century
United States

A RAILROAD MAN FOR ME

I wouldn't marry a farmer,
He's always in the dirt,
I'd rather marry a railroad man
Who wears a striped shirt!

Oh, a railroad man, a railroad man,
A railroad man for me!
I'm going to marry a railroad man,
A railroader's bride I'll be.

I wouldn't marry a blacksmith,
He's always in the black,
I'd rather marry an engineer
That throws the throttle back.

Oh, a railroad man, a railroad man.
A railroad man for me!
I'm going to marry a railroad man,
A railroader's bride I'll be.

Traditional American Folksong
nineteenth century

Rug depicting Horse, 19th century
United States

I had a little mule and his name was Jack.
I rode him on his tail to save his back.
This little mule he kicked so high,
I thought that I had touched the sky.

American Nursery Rhyme
nineteenth century

Nighthawks, 1942
Edward Hopper

MY DAD

My dad works late in a coffee shop
to put bread on the table,
he says.

It's quiet and dark,
and strange people come in.
The night is lonely,
he says.

My dad comes home late
When I am asleep.
Next year will be better,
he says.

I miss my dad.

Laura Whipple
1994

CITY BASEBALL

Crazy as white shines in summer—
shoes slapping at dusk
like fast-moving lamps—
that's how the pitcher looks
in his white shirt, almost a grown man,
winding up the ball.
And for one
minute the children
swing at it—
under the laundry-flapping sky.

Liz Rosenberg
1994

Playground in a Mill Village, 1909
Lewis Hine

BROOKLYN BRIDGE
(Jump Rope Rhyme)

Brooklyn Bridge, Brooklyn Bridge,
I walked to the middle, jumped over the
                                        edge,

The water was greasy, the water was
                                        brown
Like cold chop suey in Chinatown,

And I gobbled it up as I sank down,—
                Down—
                        Down—
                                Down—
                                        Down—

Brooklyn Bridge, Brooklyn Bridge,
I walked to the middle, looked over the
                                        edge.

But I didn't jump off, what I said's
                        not true—
I just made it up so I could scare you;
                Watch me jump!—
                        Watch me jump!—
                                Watch me jump!—
                                        BOO!

                        William Jay Smith
                        1979

Brooklyn Bridge, c. 1930
Sherril V. Schell

Western Industrial, 1955
Charles Sheeler

THE FOUNDATIONS OF AMERICAN INDUSTRY

In the Ford plant
at Ypsilanti
men named for their
fathers work at steel
machines named Bliss,
Olaffson, Smith-Grieg,
and Safety.

In the Ford plant
the generators
move quickly on
belts, a thousand now
an hour. New men
move to the belt when
the shift comes. . . .

when they walk home
they walk on sidewalks
marked W
PA 38;
their old men made
them, and they walk on
their fathers.

Donald Hall
1958

Untitled from "Pittsburgh," 1955–57
W. Eugene Smith

THE BRIDGE

Glittering bridge
curved like a harp
with your necklace of sparkling lights,
how you shine through the dark
of these silent summer nights.

Charlotte Zolotow
1987

Smog 14 Street, 1969
James Rosenquist

From Room 3003—The Shelton, New York, 1927
Alfred Stieglitz

SMOKE ANIMALS

Out of the factory chimney tall
Great black animals like to crawl.
They push each other and shove and crowd.
They nose the wind and they claw a cloud,
And they walk right out on the empty sky
With their tails all curled and their heads held high; . . .

Rowena Bastin Bennett
1968

PEOPLE WHO MUST

I painted the roof of a skyscraper.
I painted a long while and called it a day's work.
The people on the corner swarmed and the traffic cop's whistle
        never let up all afternoon.
They were the same as bugs, many bugs on their way—
These people on the go or at a standstill;
And the traffic cop a spot of blue, a splinter of brass,
Where the black tides ran around him
And he kept the street. I painted a long while
And called it a day's work.

                                        Carl Sandburg
                                        1920

Empire State Building, 1931
Lewis Hine

door

My grandmother's
Glass front door
Held a fancy pattern
Of panes, their
Heavy edges cut
On a slant: when
Sun shone through,
They scattered
Some eighty little
Flakes of rainbows
Into the room,
Walking the walls,
Glowing like fallen
Flowers on the floor;
Why don't they
Make front doors that
Way any more?

Valerie Worth
1976

Window with Bird Design, c. 1925
Edgar Miller

Mountain Scene, 1940
Torvald Arnt Hoyer

MIDWEST TOWN

Farther east it wouldn't be on the map—
    Too small—but here it rates a dot and a name.
In Europe it would wear a castle cap
    Or have a cathedral rising like a flame.

But here it stands where the section roadways meet,
    Its houses dignified with trees and lawn;
The stores hold tête-à-tête across Main Street;
    The red brick school, a church—the town is gone.

America is not all traffic lights
    And beehive homes and shops and factories;
No, there are wide green days and starry nights,
    And a great pulse beating strong in towns like these.

Ruth Delong Peterson
1954

Night Grip, 1966
Robert Rauschenberg

Whirligig entitled "America," 1938/42
Frank Memkus

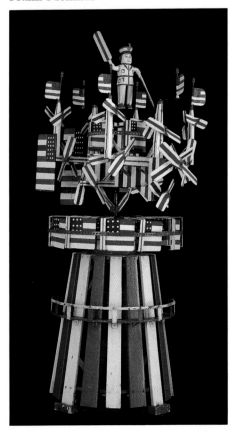

HANG OUT THE FLAG

This is Flag Day.
Hang out the flags;
Watch them rise with the breeze
And droop when it sags.
Hang out the flags.

Hang them from short poles;
Hang them from long.
See their bright colors
Shimmering strong,
Drifting along.

Flags mean our Homeland,
Country we love.
Let them sparkle in sunshine
Proudly above,
Showing our love.

James S. Tippett
1944

OUR FLAG

I love to see the starry flag
That floats above my head.
I love to see its waving folds
With stripes of white and red.
''Be brave,'' say the red stripes,
''Be pure,'' say the white.
''Be true,'' say the bright stars,
''And stand for the right.''

Author Unknown
twentieth century

Fourth of July, Jay, New York, 1958
Robert Frank

MAP OF MY COUNTRY

A map of my native country is all edges,
The shore touching sea, the easy impartial rivers
Splitting the local boundary lines. . . .
The Mississippi runs down the middle. Cape Cod. The
    Gulf.
Nebraska is on latitude forty. Kansas is west of Missouri.

When I was a child, I drew it from memory,
A game in the schoolroom, naming the big cities right. . . .

John Holmes
1963

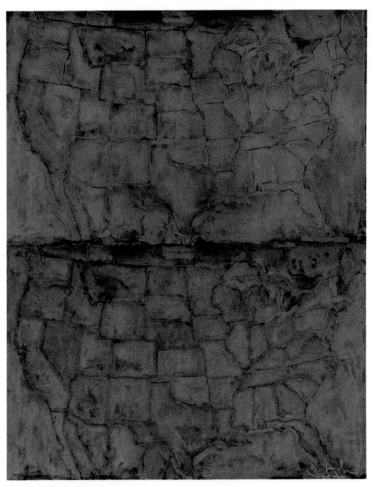

Two Maps I, 1965–66
Jasper Johns

PEOPLE

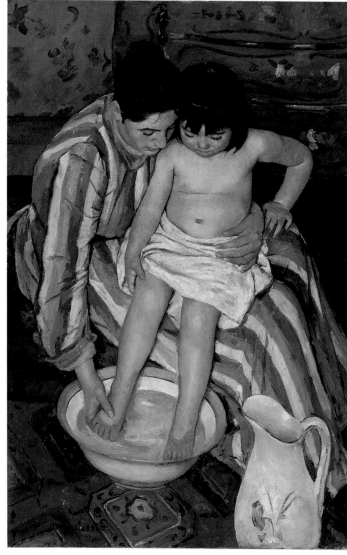

The Bath, 1891–92
Mary Cassatt

trips

eeeveryyee time
when I take my bath
and comb my hair (i mean
mommy brushes it 'til i almost cry)
and put on my clean clothes
and they all say MY
HOW NICE YOU LOOK
and i smile and say
"thank you mommy cleaned
me up"
then i sit down and mommy says
GET UP FROM THERE YOU GONNA BE DIRTY
'FORE I HAVE A CHANCE TO GET DRESSED MY SELF
and i want to tell her if you was
my size the dirt would catch
you up faster too

Nikki Giovanni
1971

TO P.J.
(2 yrs old who sed write
a poem for me in Portland, Oregon)

if i cud ever write a
poem as beautiful as u
little 2/yr/old/brotha,
i wud laugh, jump, leap
up and touch the stars
cuz u be the poem i try for
each time i pick up a pen and paper.
u. and Morani and Mungu
be our blue/blk/stars that
will shine on our lives and
makes us finally BE.
if i cud ever write a poem as beautiful
as u, little 2/yr/old/brotha,
poetry wud go out of bizness.

Sonia Sanchez
1971

Little Mother, Pittsburgh, 1909
Lewis Hine

Chicago Slums, 1911
Lewis Hine

NARCISSA

Some of the girls are playing jacks.
Some are playing ball.
But small Narcissa is not playing
Anything at all. . . .

Gwendolyn Brooks
1956

FOUR ON A SIDEWALK

TWO's a couple
THREE's a crowd,
FOUR on the sidewalk
is never allowed.

American Counting Rhyme

Chinatown, #6, date unknown
Arnold Genthe

Erroll Garner, 1960
Dennis Stock

THE WEARY BLUES

. . . With his ebony hands on each ivory key
He made that poor piano moan with melody.
　　　O Blues!
Swaying to and fro on his rickety stool
He played that sad raggy tune like a musical fool.
　　　Sweet Blues!
Coming from a black man's soul.
　　　O Blues!

Langston Hughes
1926

MOTTO

I play it cool
And dig all jive.
That's the reason
I stay alive.

My motto,
As I live and learn,
                is:
*Dig and Be Dug
In Return.*

Langston Hughes
1951

Nightlife, 1943
Archibald J. Motley, Jr.

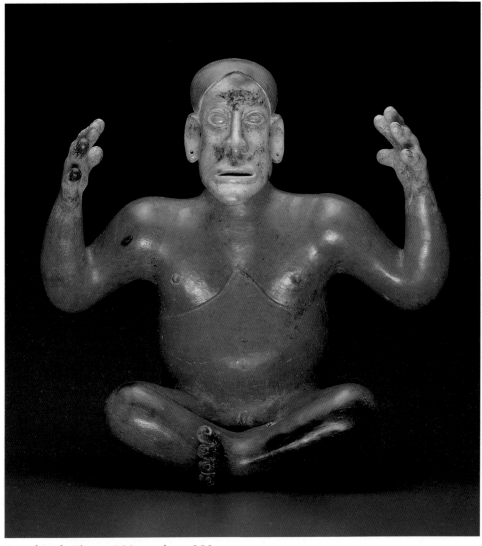

Seated Male Figure, 100 B.C./A.D. 250
Mexico, West Central Region

The true storyteller is a
TLAQUETZQUI
he says things boldly
with the lips and mouth
of an artist

The true storyteller
uses words of joy
flowers are on his lips
his language is noble

The bad storyteller
is careless
he confuses words
he swallows them
he says useless words
he has no dignity

Toltec

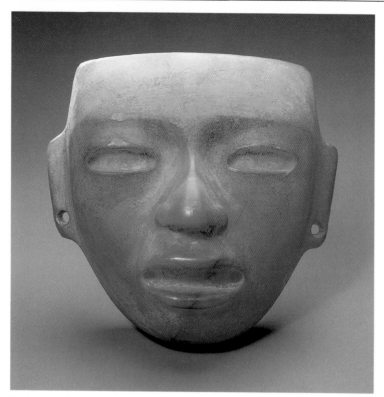

The Toltecs were wise
They conversed
with their own hearts

They played their drums
They were singers
They made songs
They guarded their songs in their memories

The Toltecs were wise
They conversed
with their own hearts.

Toltec

Votive Mask, 200/700
Mexico, Teotihuacan Culture

A voice
I will send
Hear me
The land
All over
A voice
I am sending
Hear me
I will live.

Teton Sioux

Ritual Cache Figure, 1350
Anonymous, American, Salado Culture

The beauty of wood-boys and wood-men their clear untrimmed faces,
Lumbermen in their winter camp, daybreak in the woods, stripes
      of snow on the limbs of trees, the occasional snapping,
The glad clear sound of one's own voice, the merry song, the
      natural life of the woods, the strong day's work,
The blazing fire at night, the sweet taste of supper, the talk, the
      bed of hemlock-boughs and the bear-skin; . . .

Walt Whitman
1855

A Kentucky Mountaineer, 1915
James R. Hopkins

Panel depicting Indians and Teepee, second half of 19th century
United States

DREAM SONG

as my eyes
search
the prairie
I feel the summer
in the spring.

Chippewa

A Boy Named Alligator, 1930
Kathleen Blackshear

THE PLOUGHMAN

Clear the brown path, to meet his coulter's gleam!
Lo! on he comes, behind his smoking team,
With toil's bright dew-drops on his sun-burnt brow,
The lord of earth, the hero of the plough!

First in the fields before the reddening sun,
Last in the shadows when the day is done,
Line after line, along the bursting sod,
Marks the broad acres where his feet have trod; . . .

Oliver Wendell Holmes
1849

SAILOR BOY'S SONG

Oh I am a Yankee sailor boy
My heart is wild and free
I love a roving sailor's life
As boundless as the sea
I love to watch the vessel as
She dances o'er the tide
I love to see the dolphins play
And frolic by her side
Huzza my heart it leaps for joy
To think I am a sailor boy

American Sailing Song

Stowing Sail, Bahamas, 1903
Winslow Homer

The Sunny South, 1939
Walter W. Ellison

It takes a mighty fire
to create a great people.

It takes a mighty fire
to smelt true steel;
to create and temper steel
needs patience and endurance.

The mould is not yet made, perhaps,
that can unite and make the people one.
But more important than the mould
is the temper of the steel,
the spirit of the people.

And when that steel is smelted
and when that steel is tempered
and when that steel is cast
what a people that people will be!

H. D. Carberry
1971

SPIRIT

AND YET THE EARTH REMAINS UNCHANGED

Ah, flowers that we wear!
Ah, songs that we raise! . . .
If only for one day,
let us be together, my friends!
We must leave our flowers behind us,
we must leave our songs:
and yet the earth remains unchanged.
My friends, enjoy! Friends! Enjoy!

Aztec

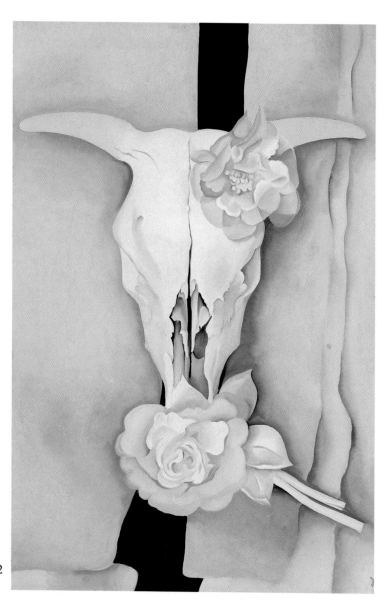

Cow's Skull with Calico Roses, 1932
Georgia O'Keeffe

SHIRT

My shirt is a token and symbol,
more than a cover for sun and rain,
my shirt is a signal,
and a teller of souls.

I can take off my shirt and tear it,
and so make a ripping razzly noise,
and the people will say,
''Look at him tear his shirt.''

I can keep my shirt on.
I can stick around and sing like a little bird
and look 'em all in the eye and never be fazed.
I can keep my shirt on.

Carl Sandburg
1920

Store Window: Bow, Hats, Heart, Shirt, 29¢, 1972
Claes Oldenburg

HELP!

Firemen, firemen!
State Police!
Victor's locked in Pop's valise!
Robert's eating kitty litter!
Doctor!
       Lawyer!
           Babysitter!

          X. J. Kennedy
           1975

RRRRRRRR, 1971
Red Grooms

IN THE EVENING

In the evening
I pull the shades
of my eyes
to see
what the night
will show me.

Siv Cedering
1979

Grayed Rainbow, 1953
Jackson Pollock

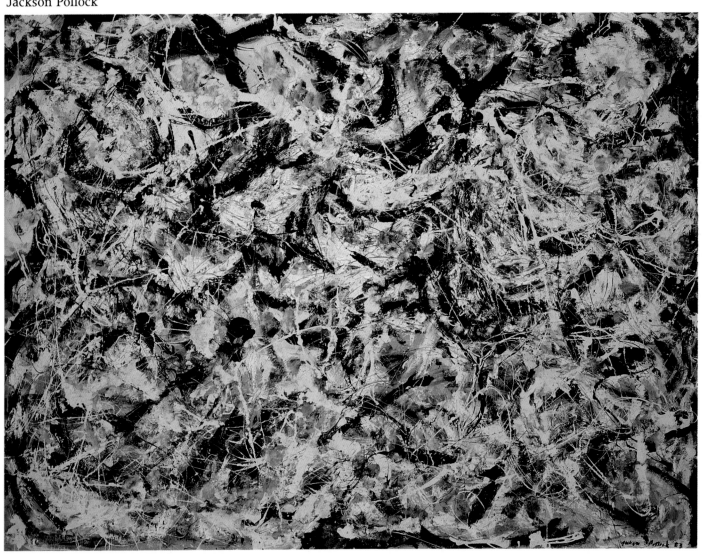

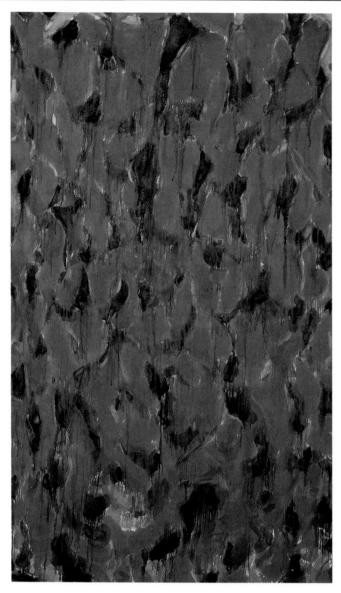

Red No. 2, 1954
Sam Francis

AT DAWN

I know I dreamed again last night.
I don't recall exactly what
Awoke me in the dead of night.
The only thing I'm certain's that
I'm grateful for the morning light.

Michael Patrick Hearn
1981

Ready to Wear, 1955
Stuart Davis

THREE/QUARTERS TIME

Dance with me . . . dance with me . . . we are the song . . . we
are the music . . .
Dance with me . . .

Dance with me . . . dance with me . . . all night long . . .
We are the music . . . we are the song . . .

Nikki Giovanni
1983

CIRCLES

The thing to draw with compasses
Are suns and moons and circleses
And rows of humptydumpasses
Or anything in circuses
Like hippopotamusseses
And hoops and camels' humpasses
And wheels on clownses busseses
And fat old elephumpasses.

Harry Behn
1949

Hatra I, 1967
Frank Stella

18 Cantos, Canto XVI, 1964
Barnett Newman

RED

Any color, so long as it's red,
    Is the color that suits me best,
Though I will allow there is much to be said
    For yellow and green and the rest;
But the feeble tints which some affect
    In the things they make or buy
Have never—I say it with all respect—
    Appealed to my critical eye.

Eugene Field
late nineteenth century

The Key, 1946
Jackson Pollock

WHY?

I don't know why I'm so crazy.
It just happens some days.
The air is full of laughing
And dancing and spinning around
And sillies and giggling
And there I am. Crazy with it.

    So I spin
    And I dance
    And I laugh
    And I giggle

And all of it whirls up together
Inside me and has to come spilling out

CRAZY.

Myra Cohn Livingston
1969

Primeval, 1962
Adolph Gottlieb

HURT

Hurt
is a dark window shade
yanked down suddenly,
slicing off the sun.
A cruel hand,
grinding helpless flowers
in its fist.
Hurt
is a hollow, hazy,
mauve and mildew feeling—
embroidered garishly
with
pricks
of
pain.

Marcie Hans
1965

KEEP A HAND ON YOUR DREAM

Keep a hand on your dream—
    Let it go too soon
And, though broad in the beam
    As a blown balloon,

It will dart all around
    Taking crazy trips,
Blowing spittle and sound
    From insulting lips.

                    X. J. Kennedy
                    1983

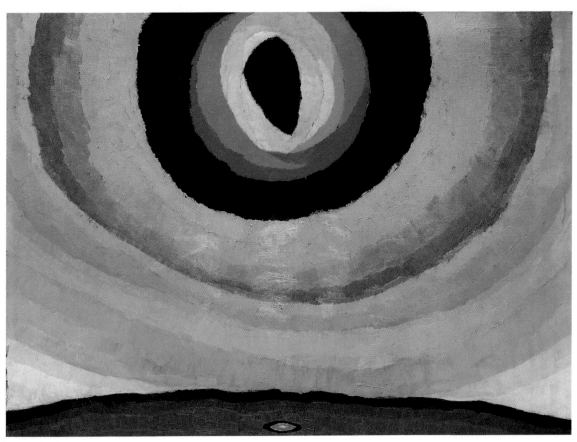

Silver Sun, 1929
Arthur Dove

Index of First Lines

A map of my native country is all edges, 48
A voice, 57
Ah, flowers that we wear!, 65
Andrew Jackson was eight feet tall., 22
Any color, so long as it's red, 71
as my eyes, 59

Begone, calm., 13
Birds and leaves disconnect in Fall, 16
Both my grandmas came from far away, 29
Brooklyn Bridge, Brooklyn Bridge, 40

Clear the brown path, to meet his coulter's, 60
Clothed in buckskin, clothed in homespun, 30
Crazy as white shines in summer—, 39

Dance with me . . . dance with me . . . we are
   the song . . . we, 70

eeeveryyee time, 51

Farther east it wouldn't be on the map—, 45
Firemen, firemen!, 67

Glittering bridge, 41

Hurt, 73

I come upon it suddenly, alone—, 18
I don't know why I'm so crazy., 72
I had a little mule and his name was Jack., 37
I know I dreamed again last night., 69
I love to see the starry flag, 47
I painted the roof of a skyscraper., 43
I play it cool, 55
I wouldn't marry a farmer, 37
if i cud ever write a, 52
In the evening, 68
In the Ford plant, 41
It takes a mighty fire, 62

Keep a hand on your dream—, 74

Last summer, 15

Most gunmen, 27
My dad works late in a coffee shop, 38
My grandmother's, 44
My home over there, my home over there, 11
My shirt is a token and symbol, 66

Not like the brazen giant of Greek fame, 28

O I'm a jolly old cowboy, 27
Ocean Spirit, 14
Oh I am a Yankee sailor boy, 61
Out of the bosom of the air, 17
Out of the factory chimney tall, 42

. . . proclaim liberty throughout, 21

Remember he was poor and country-bred;, 23

So through the night rode Paul Revere;, 24
Some of the girls are playing jacks., 53

The beauty of wood-boys and wood-men their clear
   untrimmed faces, 58
The flower-fed buffalos of the spring, 25
The thing to draw with compasses, 71
The Toltecs were wise, 57
The true storyteller is a, 56
There was a mountain, over its black roots [the deer], 17
This is Flag Day., 46
Train is a-comin', oh yes, 34
TWO's a couple, 53

We hitched up the mare and we buckled her down, 35
When I speak, now, 12
With a line and hook, 36
With company coming, 33
. . . With his ebony hands on each ivory key, 54

You have no right to trouble me, 26

Index of Poets and Artists

Aztec (traditional) 65

Behn, Harry 71
Bennett, Rowena Bastin 42
Blackshear, Kathleen 60
Book of Leviticus 21
Bourke-White, Margaret 28
Bradford, William 14
Brooks, Gwendolyn 53

Carberry, H. D. 62
Cassatt, Mary 51
Cedering, Siv 68
Chippewa (traditional) 59
Church, Frederic Edwin 12
Clift, William 13
Cole, Thomas 11

Davis, Stuart 70
Dove, Arthur 74
Dunbar, Paul Laurence 36

Ellison, Walter W. 34, 62

Field, Edward 29
Field, Eugene 71
Fisher, Aileen 33
Fisher, Aileen and Olive Rabe 30
Francis, Sam 69
Frank, Robert 35

Genthe, Arnold 53
Giovanni, Nikki 51, 70
Gottlieb, Adolph 73
Grooms, Red 67

Haida (traditional) 14
Hall, Donald 41
Hans, Marcie 73
Hearn, Michael Patrick 69
Hine, Lewis 29, 39, 43, 52, 53
Holmes, John 48
Holmes, Oliver Wendell 60
Homer, Winslow 30, 61
Hopkins, James R. 58
Hopper, Edward 38
Hoyer, Torvald Arnt 36, 45
Hughes, Langston 54, 55

Inness, George 18
Iroquois (traditional) 26

Johns, Jasper 48

Kennedy, X. J. 67, 74
Kent, Rockwell 17

Lazarus, Emma 28
Lee, Doris 33

Lindsay, Vachel 22, 25
Livingston, Myra Cohn 72
Longfellow, Henry Wadsworth 17, 24

Meigs, Mildred 23
Memkus, Frank 46
Merriam, Eve 13
Merritt, Susan 35
Mexico, Teotihuacan 57
Mexico, West Central Region, Jalisco, 56
Miller, Edgar 44
Motley, Archibald J., Jr. 55

Newman, Barnett 71

O'Keeffe, Georgia 16, 65
Oldenburg, Claes 66

Papago (traditional) 17
Peck, Robert Newton 35
Peterson, Ruth Delong 45
Pollock, Jackson 68, 72
Potthast, Edward 15

Rauschenberg, Robert 23, 46
Remington, Frederic 26, 27
Riley, James Whitcomb 18
Rivers, Larry 24
Rosenberg, Liz 39
Rosenquist, James 42
Rush, William 22

Sanchez, Sonia 52
Sandburg, Carl 43, 66
Schell, Sherril V. 40
Schick, Eleanor 15
Sertima, Ivan Van 12
Sheeler, Charles 41
Shirlaw, Walter 21
Smith, W. Eugene 41
Smith, William Jay 40
Stella, Frank 71
Stieglitz, Alfred 42
Stock, Dennis 54

Teton Sioux (traditional) 57
Tewa (traditional) 11
Tippett, James S. 46
Toltec (traditional) 56, 57
Twatchman, John Henry 17

United States 25, 34, 37, 57

Whipple, Laura 38
Whitman, Walt 58
Worth, Valerie 44

Zimmer, Paul 16
Zolotow, Charlotte 41

Notes on the Artwork

Anonymous, American, Salado culture
Ritual Cache Figure, c. 1350
Stone, wood, cotton, feathers, and pigment; h. 25¼ in.
Major Acquisitions Centennial Endowment, 1979.17a

Kathleen Blackshear (American, 1897–1988)
A Boy Named Alligator, 1930
Oil on canvas; 22 × 18 in.
Gift of Mr. and Mrs. William J. Terrell, Sr., 1991.160

Margaret Bourke-White (American, 1904–1971)
Statue of Liberty, date unknown
Silver-gelatin print; 19³/₁₆ × 15⁷/₁₆ in.
Photography Purchase Fund, 1957.130

William Bradford (American, 1823–1892)
The Coast of Labrador, 1866
Oil on canvas; 28³/₈ × 44⁵/₈ in.
Ada Turnbull Hertle Fund, 1983.529

Mary Cassatt (American, 1844–1926)
The Bath, 1891–92
Oil on canvas; 39½ × 26 in.
Robert A. Waller Fund, 1910.2

Frederic Edwin Church (American, 1826–1900)
Cotopaxi, 1857
Oil on canvas; 24½ × 36½ in.
Gift of Jennette Hamlin in memory of Mr. and Mrs. Louis Dana
Webster, 1919.753

William Clift (American, b. 1944)
Factory Butte, Utah, 1975
Silver-gelatin print; 16⅛ × 22¹⁵/₁₆ in.
Restricted gift of Anne Desloge Werner in memory of Lovis Werner II,
1987.76

Thomas Cole (American, 1801–1848)
Niagara Falls, 1830
Oil on panel; 18⁷/₈ × 23⁷/₈ in.
Friends of American Art Collection, 1946.396

Stuart Davis (American, 1894–1964)
Ready to Wear, 1955
Oil on canvas; 56¼ × 42 in.
Mr. and Mrs. Sigmund W. Kundstadter; Goodman Fund, 1956.137

Arthur Dove (American, 1880–1946)
Silver Sun, 1929
Oil and metallic paint on canvas; 21⁵/₈ × 29⁵/₈ in.
Alfred Stieglitz Collection, 1949.531

Walter W. Ellison (American, 1899–1977)
The Sunny South, 1939
Monotype on Japanese paper; 21¹/₁₆ × 16 in.
H. Carl and Nancy von Maltitz Endowment, 1990.158

Walter W. Ellison (American, 1899–1977)
Train Station, 1936
Oil on canvas; 8 × 14 in.
Charles M. Kurtz Charitable Trust and Barbara Neff and Solomon
Byron Smith funds; through prior gifts of Florence Jane Adams, Mr.
and Mrs. Carter H. Harrison, and Estate of Celia Schmidt, 1900.134

Sam Francis (American, b. 1923)
Red No. 2, 1954
Oil on Canvas; 76 × 45 in.
Restricted gift of Mr. and Mrs. James W. Alsdorf; Ada Turnbull Hertle
Fund, Edward E. Ayer in memory of Charles L. Hutchinson, Maurice
D. Galleher, Wirt D. Walker endowments, 1975.127

Robert Frank (American, b. 1924)
Fourth of July, Jay, New York, from *The Americans,* 1958
Silver-gelatin print; 13¼ × 8¾ in.
Photography Purchase Fund, 1961.942

Arnold Genthe (American, born Germany, 1869–1942)
Chinatown, #6, date unknown
Silver-gelatin print; 8⁷/₁₆ × 12½ in.
Acquired through exchange with The Library of Congress, 1952.487

Adolph Gottlieb (American, 1903–1974)
Primeval, 1962

Oil on canvas; 84 × 89¾ in.
Mary and Leigh B. Block Acquisitions Fund, 1962.774

Red Grooms (American, b. 1937)
RRRRRRRR, 1971
Color lithograph; 27¾ × 21⁷/₈ in.
Restricted gift of William E. Hartman, 1972.34

Lewis Hine (American, 1874–1940)
Chicago Slums, 1911
Silver-gelatin print; 4⁹/₁₆ × 6⁷/₁₆ in.
Acquired through exchange with George Eastman House, 1959.866

Lewis Hine (American, 1874–1940)
Empire State Building, 1931
Silver-gelatin print; 19¼ × 15⁹/₁₆ in.
Mary Leigh and Leigh B. Block Endowment, 1987.222

Lewis Hine (American, 1874–1940)
Italian Family Seeking Lost Baggage, Ellis Island, 1905
Silver-gelatin print; 7½ × 6¾ in.
Gift of David Vestal, 1965.349

Lewis Hine (American, 1874–1940)
Little Mother, Pittsburgh, 1909
Silver-gelatin print; 6¹⁵/₁₆ × 4¹⁵/₁₆ in.
Acquired through exchange with George Eastman House, 1959.861

Lewis Hine (American, 1874–1940)
Playground in a Mill Village, 1909
Silver-gelatin print; 4¹⁵/₁₆ × 6¹⁵/₁₆ in.
Acquired through exchange with George Eastman House, 1959.860

Winslow Homer (American, 1836–1910)
Mount Washington, 1869
Oil on canvas; 16¼ × 24⁵/₁₆ in.
Gift of Mrs. Richard E. Danielson and Mrs. Chauncey McCormick,
1951.313

Winslow Homer (American, 1836–1910)
Stowing Sail, Bahamas, 1903
Watercolor; 13¹⁵/₁₆ × 21¹³/₁₆ in.
Mr. and Mrs. Martin A. Ryerson Collection, 1933.1252

James R. Hopkins (American, 1877–1969)
A Kentucky Mountaineer, 1915
Oil on canvas; 32 × 36 in.
Friends of American Art Collection, 1915.561

Edward Hopper (American, 1882–1967)
Nighthawks, 1942
Oil on canvas; 33⅛ × 60⅛ in.
Friends of American Art Collection, 1942.51

Torvald Arnt Hoyer (American, born Denmark, 1872–1949)
Mountain Scene, 1940
Oil on canvas; 30¼ × 24³/₁₆ in.
Gift of Mrs. Olga Pegelow in memory of her mother Regina Dicker
Hoyer, 1986.869

Torvald Arnt Hoyer (American, born Denmark, 1872–1949)
Wheatfield, 1940
Oil on canvas; 30¼ × 24 in.
Gift of Olga Pegelow, 1949.519

George Inness (American, 1825–1894)
Our Old Mill, 1849
Oil on canvas; 29⁷/₈ × 42⅛ in.
The Goodman Fund, 1939.388

Jasper Johns (American, b. 1930)
Two Maps I, 1965–66
Lithograph; 33⅜ × 26½ in.
Gift of Albert Kunstadter Family Foundation, 1982.952

Rockwell Kent (American, 1882–1971)
Mount Equinox, Winter, 1921
Oil on canvas; 34⅛ × 44¼ in.
Gift of Gertrude V. Whitney, 1923.51

Doris Lee (American, 1905–1983)
Thanksgiving, 1935
Oil on canvas; 28⅛ × 40 in.
Mr. and Mrs. Frank G. Logan Prize Fund, 1935.313

Frank Memkus (1895–1965)
Whirligig entitled "America," 1938/42
Wood and metal, h. 80¾ in.
Restricted gift of Marshall Field, Mr. and Mrs. Robert A. Kubicek,
James Raoul Simmons, Esther Sparks, Mrs. Frank L. Sulzberger, and the
Oak Park-River Forest Associates of the Woman's Board, 1980.166

Susan Merritt (American, 1826–1879)
Fourth of July Picnic at Weymouth Landing, c. 1853
Watercolor and collage on paper; 26 × 36 in.
Gift of Elizabeth R. Vaughan, 1950.1846

Mexico, Teotihuacan Culture
Votive Mask, 200/700
Calcite; h.19 cm.
Gift of Florene May Schoenborn and Samuel A. Marx, 1958.323

Mexico, West Central Region, Jalisco, Ameca Style
Seated Male Figure, 100 B.C./A.D. 250
Ceramic; 20⅝ × 21⅞ in.
Estate of Ruth Falkenau, 1989.83

Edgar Miller (American, 1900–1993)
Window with Bird Design, c. 1925
Blue, red, yellow, and orange stained and painted glass; 27¼ × 8 in.
Mr. and Mrs. Frank G. Logan Fund, 1925.45

Archibald J. Motley, Jr. (American, 1891–1981)
Nightlife, 1943
Oil on canvas; 36 × 74¾ in.
Restricted gift of the James W. Alsdorf Memorial Fund, Mr. and Mrs.
Marshall Field, Jack and Sandra Guthman, Ben W. Heineman, Ruth
Horwich, Lewis and Susan Manilow, Beatrice C. Mayer, Charles E.
Meyer, John B. Nichols, Mr. and Mrs. E. B. Smith, Jr.; Goodman
Endowment, 1992.89

Barnett Newman (American, 1905–1970)
18 Cantos, Canto XVI, 1964
Lithograph; 17½ × 13⅝ in.
U.L.A.E. Collection, challenge grant of Mr. and Mrs. Thomas Ditt-
mer; restricted gift of supporters of the Department of Prints and
Drawings; Centennial Endowment, 1982.533

Georgia O'Keeffe (American, 1887–1986)
Cow's Skull with Calico Roses, 1932
Oil on canvas; 37⅞ × 24 in.
Gift of Georgia O'Keeffe, 1947.712

Georgia O'Keeffe (American, 1887–1986)
Yellow Hickory Leaves with Daisy, 1928
Oil on canvas; 27⅞ × 39⅞ in.
Alfred Stieglitz Collection, gift of Georgia O'Keeffe, 1965.1180

Claes Oldenburg (American, born Sweden, 1929)
Store Window: Bow, Hats, Heart, Shirt, 29¢, 1972
Lithograph; 26¾ × 22⁷⁄₁₆ in.
Gift of Mr. and Mrs. Stanley M. Freehling, 1973.499

Jackson Pollock (American, 1912–1956)
Grayed Rainbow, 1953
Oil on canvas; 72 × 96 in.
Gift of the Society for Contemporary American Art, 1955.494

Jackson Pollock (American, 1912–1956)
The Key, 1946
Oil on canvas; 59 × 84 in.
Through prior gift of Mr. and Mrs. Edward Morris, 1987.261

Edward Potthast (American, 1857–1927)
A Holiday, 1915
Oil on canvas; 30¹⁄₁₆ × 40¹⁄₁₆ in.
Friends of American Art Collection, 1915.560

Robert Rauschenberg (American, b. 1925)
Lincoln, 1958
Oil and collage on canvas; 17 × 20⅞ in.
Gift of Mr. and Mrs. Edwin E. Hokin, 1965.1174

Robert Rauschenberg (American, b. 1925)
Night Grip, 1966
Lithograph from two stones; 31⅜ × 22⅜ in.
U.L.A.E. Collection, challenge grant of Mr. and Mrs. Thomas Ditt-
mer; restricted gift of supporters of the Department of Prints and
Drawings; Centennial Endowment, 1982.1140

Frederic Remington (American, 1861–1909)
Coming Through the Rye, modeled 1902, cast 1902–09
Bronze; h. 28½ in.
George F. Harding Collection, 1982.810

Frederic Remington (American, 1861–1909)
Nothing But Cheerful Looks Followed the Bat, 1905
Oil on canvas; 27⅛ × 40¼ in.
George F. Harding Collection, 1982.784

Larry Rivers (American, b. 1923)
Once More Paul Revere, I, 1967–69
Lithograph from five stones and six plates; 28 × 39¹⁵⁄₁₆ in.
U.L.A.E. Collection, challenge grant of Mr. and Mrs. Thomas Ditt-
mer; restricted gift of supporters of the Department of Prints and
Drawings; Centennial Endowment, 1982.922

James Rosenquist (American, b. 1933)
Smog 14 Street, 1969
Lithograph from six stones; 22½ × 31 in.
U.L.A.E. Collection, challenge grant of Mr. and Mrs. Thomas Ditt-
mer; restricted gift of supporters of the Department of Prints and
Drawings; Centennial Endowment, 1982.878

William Rush (American, 1756–1833)
General Andrew Jackson, 1819
Terracotta; h. 19⅞ in.
Restricted gift of Jamee J. and Marshall Field, the Brooks and Hope
B. McCormick Foundation; Bessie Bennett, W. G. Field, Ada Turnbull
Hertle, Laura T. Magnusson, and Major Acquisitions funds, 1985.251

Sherril V. Schell (American, 1877–1964)
Brooklyn Bridge, c. 1930
Silver-gelatin print; 18⅛ × 14 in.
Gift of Jean Levy and the Estate of Julien Levy, 1988.157.75

Charles Sheeler (American, 1882–1967)
Western Industrial, 1955
Oil on canvas; 22⅞ × 29 in.
Gift of Mr. and Mrs. Leigh B. Block, 1977.12

Walter Shirlaw (American, 1838–1909)
Toning of the Bell, 1874
Oil on canvas; 40 × 30 in.
Friends of American Art Collection, 1938.1280

W. Eugene Smith (American, 1918–1978)
Untitled from *"Pittsburgh,"* 1955–57
Silver-gelatin print; 9¹⁄₁₆ × 13⁷⁄₁₆ in.
Gift of Dr. Richard L. Sandor, 1986.3112

Frank Stella (American, b. 1936)
Hatra I, 1967
Acrylic on canvas; 10 ft. × 20 ft.
Major Acquisition Fund; 1970.842

Alfred Stieglitz (American, 1864–1946)
From Room 3003—The Shelton, New York, 1927
Chloride print; 3⅝ × 4¹¹⁄₁₆ in.
The Alfred Stieglitz Collection, 1949.708

Dennis Stock (American, b. 1928)
Erroll Garner from *Jazz Street,* 1960
Original black and white; 10⁷⁄₁₆ × 13⅜ in.
Gift of the Photographer, 1963.176

John Henry Twatchman (American, 1853–1902)
Icebound, 1889/1900
Oil on canvas; 25¼ × 30⅛ in.
Friends of American Art Collection, 1917.200

United States
Panel depicting Indians and Buffalo, mid-1850s
Cotton, plain weave; engraved roller printed; 38½ × 24¼ in.
Gift of Mrs. Potter Palmer, 1949.954

United States
Panel depicting Indians and Teepee, second half of 19th century
Cotton, plain weave; engraved roller printed; 70 × 50 in.
Gift of Emily Crane Chadbourne, 1928.793

United States
Rug depicting Horse, 19th century
Linen, plain weave with cotton and wool strips of plain and twill
weaves forming "hooked" piles; 29¾ × 45⅛ in.
Bequest of William McCormick Blair, 1984.1075

United States
Rug depicting Steam Engine, 19th century
Linen, plain weave with cotton and wool strips of plain and twill
weaves forming "hooked" piles; edged with cotton, twill weave tape;
32⅛ × 61⅛ in.
Bequest of William McCormick Blair, 1984.1086

Acknowledgments

Every effort has been made to secure permission to reprint the material in *Celebrating America*. If any errors or omissions have accidently occurred, they will be corrected in subsequent editions, provided notification is sent to the publisher. Grateful acknowledgment is made to the following people for permission to reprint from previously printed material:

Harry Behn: "Circles," from *The Little Hill* by Harry Behn. Copyright 1949 by Harry Behn, renewed 1977 by Alice L. Behn. Reprinted by permission of Marian Reiner.

Rowena Bastin Bennett: "Smoke Animals," from *The Day Is Dancing and Other Poems* by Rowena Bastin Bennett. Copyright © 1968 by Rowena Bastin Bennett. Reprinted by permission of Modern Curriculum Press, Inc.

John Bierhorst: "And Yet the Earth Remains Unchanged," from *In the Trail of the Wind* by John Bierhorst. Copyright © 1971 by John Bierhorst. Reprinted by permission of Farrar, Straus & Giroux, Inc.

Gwendolyn Brooks: "Narcissa," from *Bronzeville Boys and Girls* by Gwendolyn Brooks. Copyright © 1956 by Gwendolyn Brooks Blakely. Reprinted by permission of HarperCollins Publishers.

H. D. Carberry: "It Takes a Mighty Fire . . . ," from *Breaklight: The Poetry of the Caribbean* by Andrew Salkey, ed. Copyright © 1971 by Andrew Salkey. Reprinted by permission of Doubleday, a division of Bantam Doubleday Dell Publishing Group, Inc.

Siv Cedering: "In the Evening," from *The Blue Horse*. Copyright © 1979 by Siv Cedering. Reprinted by permission of the author.

Edward Field: "Both My Grandmothers." Copyright © 1977 by Edward Field. Reprinted by permission of the author.

Aileen Fisher: "Thanksgiving Dinner," from *In One Door and Out the Other* by Aileen Fisher. Copyright © 1969 by Aileen Fisher. Reprinted by permission of HarperCollins Publishers.

Aileen Fisher and Olive Rabe: "Pioneers," from *Patriotic Plays and Programs* by Aileen Fisher and Olive Rabe. Copyright © 1956 by Aileen Fisher and Olive Rabe. Reprinted by permission of Plays, Inc., 120 Boylston Street, Boston, Massachusetts.

Toni de Gerez: "The Toltecs Were Wise . . . ," from *My Song Is A Piece of Jade, Poems of Ancient Mexico in English and Spanish,* text adapted by Toni de Gerez. English translation copyright © 1984 by Organizacion Editonial Novaro. Reprinted by permission of Little, Brown and Company.

Nikki Giovanni: "Three/Quarters Time," from *Those Who Ride the Night Winds* by Nikki Giovanni. Copyright © 1983 by Nikki Giovanni. Reprinted by permission of William Morrow & Co., Inc.

Nikki Giovanni: "trips," from *Spin A Soft Black Song* by Nikki Giovanni. Copyright © 1971, 1985 by Nikki Giovanni. Reprinted by permission of Farrar, Straus & Giroux, Inc.

Donald Hall: "The Foundations of American Industry," from *Old and New Poems* by Donald Hall. Copyright © 1990 by Donald Hall. Reprinted by permission of Ticknor & Fields/Houghton Mifflin Co. All rights reserved.

Marcie Hans: "Hurt," from *Serve Me A Slice of Moon.* Copyright © 1965 by Marcie Hans. Reprinted by permission of Harcourt Brace & Company.

Michael Patrick Hearn: "At Dawn." Copyright © 1981 by Michael Patrick Hearn. Reprinted by permission of McIntosh and Otis, Inc.

Langston Hughes: "Motto," from *The Panther and the Lash* by Langston Hughes. Copyright 1951 by Langston Hughes. Reprinted by permission of Alfred A. Knopf, Inc.

Langston Hughes: "The Weary Blues," from *Selected Poems* by Langston Hughes. Copyright 1926 by Alfred A. Knopf, Inc. and renewed 1954 by Langston Hughes. Reprinted by permission of the publisher.

X. J. Kennedy: "Help!" Copyright © 1975 by X. J. Kennedy. Reprinted by permission of Curtis Brown, Ltd.

X. J. Kennedy: "Keep A Hand on Your Dream." Copyright © 1983 by X. J. Kennedy. Reprinted by permission of the author.

Vachel Lindsay: "The Flower-Fed Buffalos," from *Going to the Stars* by Vachel Lindsay. Copyright 1926 by D. Appleton & Co., renewed 1954 by Elizabeth C. Lindsay. A Hawthorn Book. Reprinted by permission of Dutton Children's Books, a division of Penguin Books USA Inc.

Vachel Lindsay: "The Statue of Old Andrew Jackson," from *Collected Poems of Vachel Lindsay.* Copyright 1920 by Macmillan Publishing Company, renewed 1948 by Elizabeth C. Lindsay. Reprinted by permission of Macmillan Publishing Company.

Myra Cohn Livingston: "Why?" from *A Crazy Flight and Other Poems.* Copyright © 1969 by Myra Cohn Livingston. Reprinted by permission of Marian Reiner.

Mildred Meigs: "Abraham Lincoln." Reprinted by permission of C. Walter Ruckel.

Eve Merriam: "A Spell of Weather," from *A Sky Full of Poems* by Eve Merriam. Copyright © 1964, 1970, 1973 by Eve Merriam. Reprinted by permission of Marian Reiner.

Robert Newton Peck: "Four of July." Copyright © 1975 by Robert Newton Peck. Reprinted by permission of the author.

Liz Rosenberg: "City Baseball." Copyright © 1994 by Liz Rosenberg.

Sonia Sanchez: "To P.J. (2 yrs old who sed write a poem for me in Portland, Oregon)," from *It's a New Day.* Copyright © 1971 by Sonia Sanchez. Reprinted by permission of the author. *It's a New Day* published by Broadside Press.

Carl Sandburg: "People Who Must," from *Smoke and Steel.* Copyright 1920 by Harcourt Brace & Company and renewed 1948 by Carl Sandburg. Reprinted by permission of the publisher.

Carl Sandburg: "Shirt," from *Smoke and Steel.* Copyright 1920 by Harcourt Brace & Company and renewed 1948 by Carl Sandburg. Reprinted by permission of the publisher.

Eleanor Schick: "Last Summer . . . ," from *City Sun* by Eleanor Schick. Copyright © 1974 by Eleanor Schick. Reprinted by permission of Macmillan Publishing Company.

William Jay Smith: "Brooklyn Bridge," from *Laughing Time: Collected Nonsense* by William Jay Smith. Copyright © 1990 by William Jay Smith. Reprinted by permission of Farrar, Straus & Giroux, Inc.

Laura Whipple: "My Dad." Copyright © 1994 by Laura Whipple.

Valerie Worth: "door," from *Still More Small Poems* by Valerie Worth. Copyright © 1978 by Valerie Worth. Reprinted by permission of Farrar, Straus & Giroux, Inc.

Paul Zimmer: "Zimmer in Fall," from *The Zimmer Poems* by Paul Zimmer. Copyright © 1976 by Paul Zimmer. Reprinted by permission of the author. *The Zimmer Poems* published by Dryad Press.

Charlotte Zolotow: "The Bridge," from *Everything Glistens and Everything Sings, New and Selected Poems* by Charlotte Zolotow. Copyright © 1987 by Charlotte Zolotow. Reprinted by permission of Harcourt Brace & Company.